The Pied Piper of

HAMELIN

The Pied Piper of HAMELIN

Illustrated by *Drahos Zak* Retold by *Robert Holden*

Houghton Mifflin Company
Boston 1998

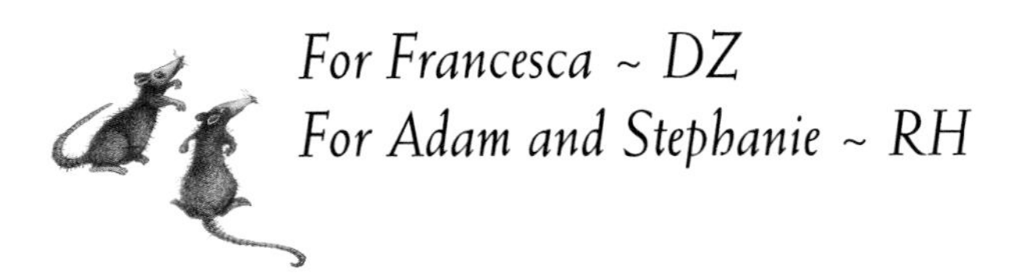

For Francesca ~ DZ
For Adam and Stephanie ~ RH

~ The illustrator gratefully acknowledges
the support of the Australia Council.

First American edition 1998
Originally published in Australia as an Angus&Robertson book by
HarperCollins*Publishers* Pty Limited
http://www.harpercollins.com.au

Walter Lorraine (wl) Books

Library of Congress Cataloguing-in-Publication Data:
Holden, Robert.
The pied piper of Hamelin / retold by Robert Holden
with illustrations by Drahos Zak.
p. cm.
Summary: The Pied Piper pipes the village free of rats,
and when the villagers refuse to pay him for the service he exacts a terrible revenge.
ISBN 0-395-89918-4
1. Pied Piper of Hamelin (Legendary character)--Legends.
[1. Pied Piper of Hamelin (Legendary character)--Legends. 2. Folklore--Germany--Hameln.]
I. Zak, Drahos, ill. II. Title.
PZ8.1.H7355Pi 1998
398.2'0943'02
[E]--DC21 97-33221
CIP
AC

Printed in China.

10 9 8 7 6 5 4 3 2 1

Hamelin Town was a town divided.
Rats and men lived side by side.
And where the difference truly lay
Some say was undecided!

Rats by day
and rats by night,
Ate their fill,
put all to flight.
Dogs were chased,
cats fled the scene.
Babies were bitten
and mothers screamed.

People were even
afraid to doze . . .

For fear
the rats
would
nibble
their
toes!

Enough was enough, they called a meeting,
The whole town gathered to voice their woes.
But above all their noise, above all the bleating,
All that was heard was rats squeak-squeaking!

The crowd grew angry, the crowd got mad.
They vowed they would give up all that they had.
Their most treasured possessions, the town's greatest riches,
To remove all the rats – they'd even use witches!

Then across all this clamour there fell one clear tune
Like peace after wartime, like roses in bloom,
And into the town that begged for some magic . . .

No
witches
arrived,
nothing
evil
or
tragic.

Instead in the square
stood a figure of wonder
Who without any pause,
without any blunder,
Proceeded to round up the rats!

He piped a sweet tune
that caused rats to dance,
To pick up their tails,
to scamper,
to prance.

It promised rat pleasures, they needn't say please,
It promised an endless supply of fine cheese!

Hamelin was free, the future looked brighter,
But after the tune you must pay the Piper.

The crowd had seen magic, yet after they cheered,

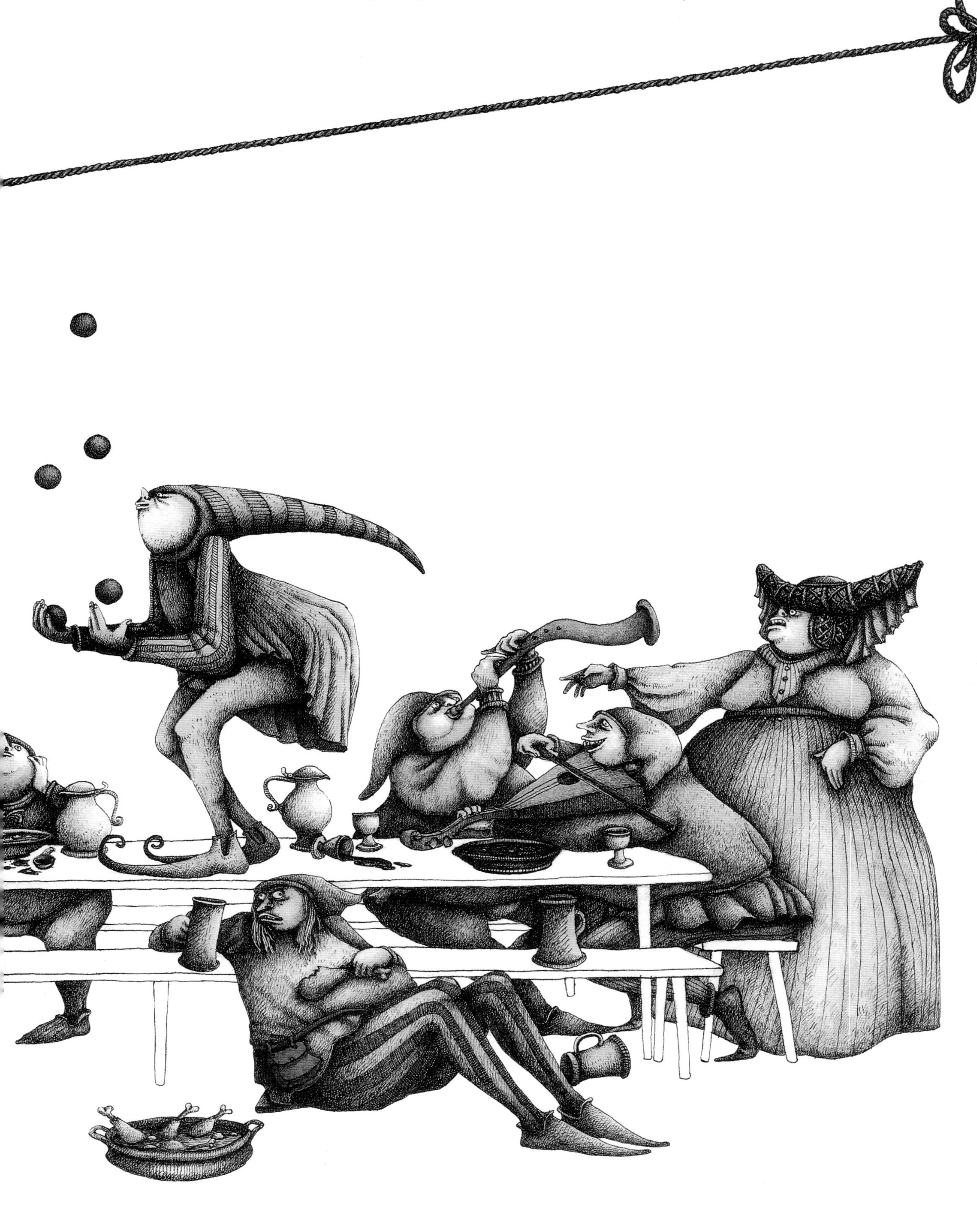

Their
own
rat-like
nature
was
shown
in
their
greed.

"What?
Give all we have,
the town's greatest riches!
You'd be lucky to get
a new pair of britches!"

The Piper stood still,
and saw that
these creatures
had nothing
of kindness
nor truth in
their features.

And looking beyond them he spurned all their gold,
Their sweetest riches could never be sold.
They shone in the eyes of girls and of boys,

That was their treasure, their greatest of joys.
The townspeople stood quite unable to credit
Their children were leaving to pay off the debit.

The Piper played once,
now he played for them twice,
And the children saw visions,
they beheld Paradise.

"You people of Hamelin
had nothing but curses,
Your hearts are now empty,
but full are your purses."

The
children
left
singing
for
a
future
much
brighter.

And thus Hamelin paid
for the tunes of the Piper.